Artesian Press

D0971024

MATCH POINT

ROBIN CRUISE

Artesian Press

P.O. Box 355 Buena Park, CA 90621

Take Ten Books
Sports

Other Take Ten Themes:
Mystery
Adventure
Disaster
Chillers
Thrillers
Fantasy

Project Editor:Liz Parker
Assistant Editor: Carol Newell
Cover/Text Illustrator:Fujiko
Cover Designer: Tony Amaro
©2001 Artesian Press

ISBN 1-58659-035-9

Chapter 1

Emily Wilson had never been good at sports.

Her mother said that wasn't true. She said it *couldn't* be true because there were so many good athletes in the family.

Emily's Uncle John had played semi-pro baseball. Her Aunt Katie still swam all the way across the lake every summer, even though she was almost 50. Emily didn't see her dad very often. He had moved to another state after the divorce, but she knew he still played softball every summer. Once he ran a marathon, 26.2 miles. Emily could not imagine running that far. She had kept the photograph of her dad crossing the finish line as a reminder that such a thing was possible.

It didn't help that sports were so easy for Emily's brothers. Andrew played basketball every winter. He was co-captain of the team and the starting forward. Henry was on the ski team; he had a second-place trophy for some juniors' slalom race. Both of them played soccer in the spring and baseball in the summer.

Even Emily's mom could make a basket when she and the boys were shooting hoops out back against the garage. But not Emily. She couldn't even hit the backboard. Every time her mom brought up sports, Emily said that riding her bike over to the library should count for something.

Every summer it was the same old story. Emily had to pick some sport to play for six weeks. She would rather just hang out at the mall or in the park with the other kids, but her mom said,

"No way."

Emily hoped that maybe her mom would forget about sports this summer. She had been very busy at work. Besides, it seemed like they never had enough money, so maybe this summer her mom wouldn't be able to pay for her to take lessons.

It didn't turn out that way....

Early one morning in late May, Mrs. Wilson sent the boys off to school on their bikes and then sat down to have breakfast with Emily. When she pulled out a summer catalog from the YMCA, Emily knew what was coming.

"So," Mrs. Wilson said, "what's it going to be this summer, Emily? Look, they have swimming and volleyball. Karate. And gymnastics!" She sounded very cheery.

Emily sighed. "Mom, I've done them all," she said. "You know I'm a lousy swimmer—I can barely float. I'd never make the team. I can't even do a cartwheel. I don't like volleyball because it hurts my wrists. Can't we just skip it this summer? Blanca doesn't do sports. And besides, how are you going to pay for it?"

Mrs. Wilson kept right on talking. "Emily, you're not Blanca, and I hope you haven't forgotten the rules: one hour of athletics for every hour of TV," she said. "You're not going to flop around all day watching that junk. Everyone needs fresh air, sunshine and exercise. You know what they say, 'Healthy mind, healthy body.'"

Mrs. Wilson was still talking when Emily cleared her place and rinsed her cereal bowl.

"Emily, today's the last day to sign up. Do you want to choose or should I?"

Emily knew she had no choice: There was no way she could get through the long, hot summer without television. She walked back to the table and asked to see the catalog. Opening it in front of her, she took a deep breath. Then she put one hand over her eyes and began to flip through the pages with the other. With the catalog laying flat on the table, she pointed to the page in front of her and uncovered her eyes.

"Tennis, Mom," she said. "Sign me up for tennis lessons."

Mrs. Wilson sounded very surprised.

"Why Emily, what a good idea," she said. "I think you'll be very good at tennis. You're so tall. That should help. And fast. And you like geometry—that should help you figure out all of those angles for the ball hitting the court. I'll sign you up today. Six weeks of tennis lessons. And look! You get to go for two whole hours, three mornings a week, for just thirty-six dollars. Maybe you should do both sessions."

Emily was getting a headache just thinking about it. She walked out of the house and waited silently in the car for her mother to drive her to school.

Chapter 2

Emily's first tennis lesson was on a Wednesday. Her mom dropped her off with her bike, and she found her way to the two hard-surface courts at the west end of the YMCA. Afterwards she could have lunch at the snack bar and hang out at the pool until Andrew came by on his bike at 1:30 to ride home with her.

There were just eight kids in the class and Blanca was one of them! She looked mad, but Emily was glad to see her anyway. The teacher was tan and smiled a lot. At 9:15 she whistled loudly through her fingers and held her racket high in the air.

"Yo!" she said. "My name is Suzy,

and are we going to play some tennis or what? Tennis is a great game, and I know you'll love it as much as I do. 'Love,' by the way, is an important word in tennis—but not the smoochy kind. Anyway, before we get started you have to know the most important rule: FUN COMES FIRST!

"No matter what, that's the Number One rule for the next six weeks," Suzy said. "Don't forget it. So what are we waiting for? Let's play some tennis."

She lined all eight of them up along a white line at the back of one of the courts.

"This," Suzy said, sweeping her racket along the line at their feet, "is the baseline. You can think of it as home base, because most of the time this is where you want to be.

"For right now, I want each of you to take a swing when I drop a ball in front of you. If you've taken lessons before or you think you know something about tennis, FORGET ALL THAT NOW! And remember Suzy-Q's Tennis Rule Number Two: RELAX. If you have fun and relax, you'll be a natural. So here we go...."

Emily could feel her heart begin to pound. She had hung back when everyone else lined up along the baseline. She watched nervously as Suzy made her way down the line toward her. She dropped a ball so that it would bounce at waist-level in front of each student.

Suzy stopped at the boy in front of Emily.

"Yo!" she said. "What's your name?"

Emily watched as he shifted his weight from foot to foot, but he spoke so quietly that she couldn't hear his name.

"Was that Eric?" Suzy said, bending closer to the boy.

He nodded mutely.

"Well, Eric, you're going to have to

speak up or you'll get lost in the crowd around here. Ever played any tennis?"

Eric shrugged and muttered, "A little. My dad and I used to play, but he's too busy now." He shrugged again.

"So, Eric," Suzy said, "let's see what you can do."

Suzy dropped a ball in front of him, and Emily held her breath as she watched. The ball made a solid plunk as he hit it squarely in front of him, the weight of his body moving slowly forward and through the ball. Somebody whistled as the ball blazed over the net, barely skimming the court a few inches inside the baseline on the other side.

Suzy turned to Eric and said, "Awesome."

Even Emily could see that he was still smiling when it was her turn to hit the ball. That was easier said than done. The little voice inside her head was still talking—"Have fun. Relax. Racket back. Weight forward."—long after Emily had swung and missed the ball. Suzy didn't flinch.

"Let's try it again," she said, bouncing a ball in front of Emily.

Emily took a breath, closed her eyes—and swung as hard as she could. When she opened her eyes she was surprised to see Eric and the rest of the class looking far off into the distance. Her ball had cleared the net and the fence, and it was still rolling across the parking lot toward the street.

"It's my mother's fault," she stammered. "I don't like tennis. I'm no good at sports. I …"

She felt Suzy's hand on her shoulder.

"Emily," Suzy said. "You've got a lot of power there. We've got six weeks to tune it up a little, but when we do— WATCH OUT!"

Suzy lined them all up again and stood in front of the group.

"We're going to take it nice and

slow," she said. "Not too much information too soon or you'll feel swamped. First, we'll take a look at the most basic stroke: the forehand. The forehand and its counterpart, the backhand are the heart of your game, and once you've mastered them, you're on your way to good tennis.

"In general, stand with your feet about shoulder-width apart. Keep your head up and your weight forward on the balls of your feet so that turning is just a quick, simple pivot. Keep your racket back and meet the ball out in front. Follow through, moving your weight forward. Got it?"

Emily and the other kids looked at each other. Nobody said a word.

"The trick is to control the motion—no wild swings," Suzy continued. "Eric, you may want to drop your racket head down when you bring your racket back so that you loop up and through the ball. That will give you more power and put a little zip on the ball."

Suzy moved through the steps again and again, with her back to her students so they could practice along with her. She made it look simple, and each time she hit the ball it lifted easily over the net, bouncing deep on the far side of the court. She split the group into four pairs and had them take turns bouncing balls to each other. Emily and Eric were partners. He kept his head down and didn't speak until Emily smacked her first ball low and hard across the net.

"That's it!" Eric said as the two of them watched the ball bounce off the baseline on the other side of the court. "Now do it again. Like Suzy said, the trick is to meet the ball out in front of you."

Emily surprised Eric and herself when she hit three balls in a row, each one low and deep. The first ball she tossed toward Eric bounced up and hit him on the side of his head. He just grinned, and Emily bounced him another ball. He did exactly what Suzy had told him to do. Emily was impressed by his smooth, steady swing.

When Suzy called "Time out!" for a juice break at 10:00, Emily and Blanca huddled together in the cool shade.

"Lucky you," Blanca said as they stretched out on the grass.

Emily was hot and tired.

"What do you mean lucky me?" she said. "I stink."

"Yeah," Blanca said, "but you'll get better and besides, like Suzy said, he's awesome!"

"*Who's* awesome?"

Blanca stood up and shook her head.

"Emily, open your eyes! Eric is totally cool. Hey, this could be your love match!"

Emily could feel herself blush. Maybe it was just the heat—or all the things she had to remember about tennis. The class spent the next hour inside, and Emily was glad to be in the air-conditioned gym. It wasn't even noon, but she could tell the day was going to be a scorcher.

Chapter 3

After the juice break, Suzy had everyone sit in a semi-circle around her. She told the kids to hold up their rackets in front of them.

"Look," she said. "Tennis rackets come in different grip sizes, weights, colors—even two different 'head' sizes." With one index finger, she outlined the rounded, strung part of the racket.

"The more you play tennis," Suzy said, "the more important it will become to have a racket that feels just right to you. The strings should be strung at just the right tension, so that you can sense exactly what will happen when you connect with the ball."

Suzy continued, laying her palm flat

against the center of the strings criss-crossing her racket head. "This is known as the 'sweet spot.' Aim to hit the ball from the sweet spot every time and you'll be fine. If you slash and swat at the ball, you'll end up bonking it with the frame or some other part of the racket. Trust me, that won't be a pretty sight. The sweet spot is your ticket to glory."

Emily had been furiously taking notes. She was beginning to feel over-whelmed.

"Any questions?" Suzy asked.

Like the other kids around her, Emily was silent.

"Okay then," Suzy said. "We're go-ing to concentrate on the forehand the rest of this week and next. On Friday we'll take a closer look at the court and how it's set up. Believe me, all those white lines make perfect sense.

"For now, just remember that the thing that counts BIG TIME on the tennis court—along with coordination, being ready at all times and playing smart—is stamina. So let's start building up your strength and your lungs today. Ten laps around the courts—and make 'em quick!"

Blanca glowered at Emily and said, "She's got to be kidding. Ten laps?"

Emily was already out the door and jogging toward the courts. Stamina was the one thing she knew she had plenty of; she figured she had built it up during all those years chasing after or running away from her brothers.

Emily had been disappointed to wake up to the sound of a steady rain on Friday, but Suzy had said there would be tennis lessons as scheduled, rain or shine. All the other kids were already in the gym by the time her mom dropped her off at the YMCA.

Suzy waved at her with her racket and motioned for her to join the group of kids seated on the floor. They were looking at a large diagram of a tennis court.

"Glad you could make it, Emily," she called. "We're talking about tennis courts and what all of these white lines have to do with the game."

Emily peeled off her windbreaker and sat down next to Blanca.

Suzy pointed to the diagram with her racket and began to explain all the white lines and boxes laid out on the green surface of the court.

"A lot of the hard courts people play on today are painted green," Suzy said. "When the game was invented in 1873, people played on grass courts. I guess painting the courts green makes them look a little like grass. Really, when the game was invented by a man named Major Walter Clopton Wingfield, it was called 'Sphairistike.'"

"*Gesundheit!*" Eric quipped, and Suzy began to laugh along with everyone else.

Blanca poked Emily in the ribs.

"What'd I tell you?" she said. "He's a crack-up *and* cute!"

Suzy continued explaining the basics of the game. "Right now we're talking about singles play; doubles is a different kind of game. So for the time being, just pay attention to these boundaries," Suzy said, her racket tracing around the court. "The court is 72 feet long, baseline to baseline—36 feet on either side of the net. And another 27 feet from sideline to sideline for singles—or 31 1/2 feet across for doubles. That's almost 1,000 square feet to cover with two feet and one racket. You can see why speed and stamina tend to separate the winners from the losers in tennis."

"Look," Mark said, pointing out the glass doors, "the sun came out."

Suzy looked at her watch. "You're right," she said. "Okay, it's 10:45. Just enough time left …"

All the kids in the class looked at each other.

"For what?" Mark said at last.

"What do you mean, 'For what?'" Suzy roared. "For stamina, of course! Get moving."

Chapter 4

So it went for the next month, as Emily's summer settled into a predictable rhythm: tennis lessons three mornings a week, lazy afternoons at the pool with friends, picnic suppers in the back yard with her mom and brothers, long bike rides by herself in the evenings and occasional bus rides to the mall with Blanca.

Emily was surprised to discover that there wasn't much time for television— and even more surprised that she didn't miss it a bit. Most nights she was so tired that she was sound asleep by 10:30. That was probably because she was playing a lot more tennis than she had imagined. It wasn't the 'love match' Blanca had teased her about at the very first lesson, but she and Eric had struck up a friendship that brought them to the YMCA courts even when they weren't taking lessons.

After the first two lessons, Emily had decided to take advantage of the free time (included in the price of lessons) on the YMCA's ball machine. When she switched on the machine the first Tuesday after her lessons began, the balls started to shoot out at her so furiously that there was no way she could keep up with them.

She was fiddling helplessly with the speed control when she was startled to feel someone tapping lightly on her back.

"Maybe I could help," Eric said quietly. "You looked a little frantic out there."

He easily adjusted the speed, and the balls began to pop out of the machine at a more reasonable pace. Emily was irritated to feel herself blush.

"Yeah," she said, striding back to the baseline. "This thing is kind of wild—I didn't hit one ball."

Eric shrugged.

"Might as well try it again," he said. "Uh, remember what Suzy said about getting your racket back first thing. That always helps me."

And so Emily did. She swatted and batted the first dozen balls, but slowly worked her stroke into a steadier groove as she lifted ball after ball over the net. She was sweaty and breathless by the time the last ball shot out of the machine.

"Your turn," she said to Eric after the two of them had retrieved the last balls from the far corners of the court. They reloaded the machine, which he adjusted to a faster speed.

Emily shook her head as she watched him.

"So that's how it's done," she

thought to herself, following the slow, graceful loop of his racket—first dropping low behind him, pushing surely through the ball and finishing high out in front of him.

"Control," Emily said as she stooped to pick up the balls at her feet. "The less wasted motion, the more control on the ball. Somehow I've got to make my stroke look as easy as Eric's."

Emily realized that she was beginning to like tennis. Her mom had been right, geometry turned out to be a part of the game—and geometry was her favorite subject. She liked the basic logic of angles and clean, hard edges. Each time Suzy demonstrated basic causes and effects in tennis, the logic made more and more sense.

The stroke, Emily began to understand, does not really change much— it's the player's position and the position of the racket at the moment of impact, together with the follow-through, that determines how fast, how deep and how wide each shot will be.

Before long, Emily grasped the idea that tennis is both a mental and a *physical* game—and that playing smart can help make up for imperfect strokes and other weaknesses.

Yes, it was all starting to make perfect sense.

Suzy had concentrated on the basics for a full month.

Emily and the other kids in the class had sweated through hours of drills. She could hit a forehand and the quick, choppy punch shot at the net that Suzy called a "volley." She could hit a "lob," the slow, vertical stroke that lifted the ball high and deep into the opposite court. She even had a sense of the basic motion of the serve—and occasionally, with total concentration, she managed to serve the ball into the right box.

The basics of the game were coming together for her, with one exception: Emily could not hit a backhand.

No matter what Emily attempted, the result was the same: The ball either bounced a few feet in front of her and rolled into the net, or it soared skyward and landed well out of bounds.

The other kids had quickly picked up on Emily's weakness. The few times Suzy had them play for points, her opponent had immediately tried to hit to Emily's backhand. She understood that playing off of her weakness was good tennis; there wasn't anything mean about it.

Eventually, she had all but given up on the shot. When she sensed that a ball would be returned to her backhand, her impulse was to run to a position on the court where she could hit her forehand. The result was that Emily inevitably found herself on the defensive—and spent much of her time struggling to regain control and catch her breath.

Her mother had been shocked to find Emily packing up her tennis gear soon after dawn on the Tuesday of her last week of classes.

"Emily," she said suspiciously, "what's gotten into you? I know I encouraged you to get some exercise this summer, but look at you. You've got tennis magazines piled up in your room, and I can't walk through one room in the house without tripping over tennis balls."

Emily didn't have time to argue with her mother—she had just four days to figure out how to hit a backhand before the doubles tournament Suzy had planned as a final for the class on Saturday.

"Mom," she said as she headed out the back door, "don't blame me. Remember, I didn't want to play tennis."

She could hear her mother still jabbering away in the kitchen as she headed off on her bike in the cool morning air.

Chapter 5

She had been hitting away at the ball machine for more than an hour when she saw Eric stroll up to the court. She liked the easy way he moved and his shy smile. Even when it was just the two of them on the court, he didn't really say much. Still, she felt comfortable with him and, more than anything, she appreciated his sense of humor. He wasn't stuck up and he didn't ever brag, even though he must have known that he was much, much better than everyone else in the class.

"Still having trouble with the backhand?" Eric said after watching her swat balls for a few minutes.

"Yeah," Emily sighed. "I know just

what to do, but I just can't get it."

"I guess that's what they call a mental block," Eric said. "Just don't think about it."

"Easier said than done," Emily replied. "Every time I try *not* to think about it, I end up thinking about it *more.* Then I get really freaked and do something dumb. Like that."

Emily watched in dismay as yet another ball rolled into the net.

"Keep hitting and let me think a minute," Eric said.

Nothing much changed. Emily managed to get every fourth or fifth ball over the net with a weak punch. Eric stood back for a few minutes and then joined Emily on the court.

"Maybe it would help to watch me hit a few," he said.

And so Emily stood by as he hit ball after ball over the net and deep into the opposite court.

"You know," she said, "from here

your backhand looks a lot like Blanca's forehand. It makes sense since Blanca's a lefty. Her forehand is pretty much your backhand. Move over, let me try something."

Emily positioned herself in front of the ball machine for a backhand shot. She totally missed the first three balls but connected solidly with the fourth ... and the fifth and the sixth. Her stroke wasn't perfect and the shots were a little short and wobbly, but for the first time Emily had a sense of what a backhand should feel like.

She was grinning happily when Eric called out to her, "Hey, I think you've got it! What did you do?"

"Forehand!" Emily replied. "I'm thinking forehand with my left hand and what that should look like even though I'm really hitting a backhand with my right hand. Does that make sense?"

Eric shrugged but grinned back at

her.

"I don't know if it makes sense," he said, "but if it works for you, who cares? Hit a few more."

When Eric asked if she wanted to ride bikes over to the deli for breakfast, Emily eagerly agreed. He ordered three waffles, two fried eggs and a large orange juice—and he looked shocked when Emily said she'd have the same.

"Heck," Eric said, "most girls eat like birds these days. Makes me feel like I'm a real chow-hound or something. It's nice to see a girl with a good appetite for once. Like Suzy says, if you're going to play good tennis, you've got to be strong."

"Yeah," Emily said, "and smart, too."

Eric didn't say anything, and Emily suddenly felt as though she had said something wrong. She thought maybe she should change the subject.

"So," she said at last, gathering up

her courage, "I'll bet you already have a partner for the doubles tournament on Saturday."

Eric looked gloomy.

"Nah," he said with a sigh. "I'm not playing."

Emily felt her heart sink.

"Not playing?" she said with disbelief. "That can't be true. Besides, everyone else already has a partner and I was kind of hoping ..."

Eric looked at her.

"To borrow your line," he said. "I stink."

"Oh, I get it," Emily replied. She could feel herself getting angry. "This is a joke. Well, I don't think it's very funny. Just because you know you're the very best player in the whole class, you say you stink. That's what you do instead of bragging that you're so good. It's not funny at all to say you stink—it's dumb. I think ..."

"Hey, calm down," Eric interrupted.

"I know I don't stink at tennis. It's not tennis I'm worried about. I stink at math."

"Emily, I'm so stupid," he moaned. "I can't figure out how to keep score. I'm in remedial math, and it's always been really hard for me. Sports are easy, *especially* tennis for some reason. But how can I hope to play tennis if I can't keep score?"

Eric looked miserable and Emily was ashamed to admit that her first impulse was to laugh. He can't keep score? But instead she nodded like it was no big deal.

"Perfect," she said after thinking for a few moments. "You help me get my backhand in a groove by Saturday and I'll tutor you in scoring. Deal?"

"Deal," Eric said just as their enormous breakfasts arrived. They both ate every bite.

Chapter 6

"You mean to tell me you spent four hours hitting off that ball machine today?" Emily's mother said at dinner that night.

"Yeah, more or less," Emily replied. "Eric says the more backhands I hit before Saturday, the more comfortable I'll be with the stroke."

Andrew and Henry looked at each other across the table.

"*Eric?*" Andrew said with a smirk. "Emily, you didn't tell us *a guy* was involved in all of this."

"Yeah," Henry teased. "No wonder our baby sister is suddenly so interested in tennis. Could this be your *love* match?"

"Boys, stop that teasing this minute," Mrs. Wilson insisted, but Emily had already cleared her place and left the room.

She stormed out the back door, saying that she was headed for the library.

"Oh, the library?" Andrew called after her. "Will *Eric* be at the library?"

As it turned out, he was. They had agreed to meet there so that Emily could explain how points add up in a tennis match. He was waiting on the steps and waved when Emily rode up on her bike. The two of them decided to chat outside, where it was cool.

"Hey, Eric," Emily said. "I don't have much time. I have to be home by 8:30 to see today's Wimbledon highlights, but I don't think this will take long."

"I don't know about that—it's all foggy to me," Eric replied. "'Love' and 'advantage in' and 'out' and all that. I just don't get it."

"Yeah, it's definitely weird and I don't know who the heck made up the crazy scoring, but for now forget about all that. Just think of scoring as four points—the first player to four wins the game. It gets tricky because you can't win a game by just one point; you have to be two points ahead to win."

"Four points?" Eric said, confused.

"Right. But instead of 1, 2, 3, and 4, the points are 15, 30, 40, and game."

"Fifteen, 30, 40, and game—1, 2, 3, and 4," Eric repeated.

"You've got it. See, it's easy," Emily said with a smile.

"Well, yeah, it doesn't make any sense, but I get the four points okay. It's all that 'advantage in' and 'advantage out' stuff that's really confusing."

"Uh-huh," Emily agreed. "That is really weird, but I guess it's just the British way of saying who's ahead. When you're serving and the score gets to 40-40—remember, sometimes they call that 'deuce'—if you win the point, then it's 'advantage in.' If you lose the point on your serve, then it's 'advantage out.' One player has to win at least six games to win the set. And, finally, the deciding point in the match is called the 'match point.' Men play six sets in a match, and women play four."

"Okay, okay," Eric sighed. "Advantage in, advantage out, game, set, match—but why the deuce does 'deuce' keep popping up?"

"Every time the score is tied, it's called 'deuce,'" Emily replied.

Eric was quiet for a long time.

"I know," Emily said. "Let's pretend we're scoring a game. You're serving and I win the first point. What's the score?"

"Hmphh!" Eric said with a grin. "I'd just hit it to your backhand, but if somehow you managed to win the first point it would be 0 to 1. That's 15 to love, right?"

"Wrong, but close," Emily said. "Remember, when you're serving, you always call your score first."

"Okay, let's see. Love-15."

Emily smiled. "You've got it!"

Chapter 7

Saturday morning was clear and surprisingly cool.

Emily was up and dressed before sunrise. She had touched up her shoes the night before, and she had even ironed her crisp white shorts and the mesh shirt her mother had bought her for her birthday. Suzy had told them that for a lot of players, looking good was part of the mental game.

Emily was dressed and ready to go but still had three hours to kill before she could even think about heading for the YMCA to warm up. She was in the kitchen flipping through a magazine when her mother wandered downstairs. That was *very* unusual—most Saturdays her mom didn't even get out of bed before 8:00. It was her one day of the week to sleep in, which usually meant that Emily and the boys were in charge of breakfast.

"Hey, Em," her mother said foggily, reaching for the coffee can. "Big day, huh?"

Emily didn't want to think about it. She and Eric had spent every spare minute the past three days hitting tennis balls and planning their strategy. They had agreed from the start that as a doubles team their best hope was to maximize their individual strengths. Eric had a strong, consistent serve and was comfortable playing the net. Emily had become more and more confident in her groundstrokes and was content to hang back at the baseline. They had agreed that the sooner Eric could get to the net, the better their chances for taking the offense and winning the point.

Emily had that queasy feeling she

often got while waiting in line to board the roller coaster.

"Ah, no big deal," she said to her mother without looking up from the magazine. "It's just a class tournament."

Mrs. Wilson was quiet for a long time. She poured herself a cup of coffee, then sat down at the kitchen table with Emily.

"You know," she said, "I don't want to make a big deal out of all this, but I want you to know how proud I am of you for really concentrating on tennis this summer. Seems to me you've grown a lot, Em—and I don't just mean you're three inches taller than you were last summer!"

Emily shrugged. "Well, I do like it," she said. "And that surprises me as much as it does you. But, Mom, can you do me a favor? Don't tell Andrew and Henry about today. They keep asking all of these questions, and I'm already super nervous."

Her mom smiled. "Don't worry," she said. "I've got plans for those two today—they haven't mowed the lawn or pulled a weed in two weeks. If they need their allowance for that dance tonight, they'll be plenty busy today.

"Now, how about some breakfast? Seems to me a big breakfast could pay off out there on the courts!"

Emily ate a huge amount, but she felt light and energized by the time she got to the courts. She had convinced her mom to let her ride her bike but had said it would be okay if Mrs. Wilson came to watch her play.

Suzy had explained the ground rules for the tournament early in the week: First thing, she would split the four pairs into groups of four each for a full set of doubles. The two losing teams would follow-up with a set, and then the two winning pairs would compete in the class finals.

After a shaky start, Emily and Eric

had no problem taking their first set 6-3 from Lauren and Bret. Emily's heart sank when she realized they would face Blanca and Mark in the finals.

"Uh-oh," she said to Eric as the two of them watched Lauren and Bret square off against Megan and Sam. "I think we're in trouble. Mark has a killer serve and Blanca has more stamina than anyone. We haven't got a chance."

Eric frowned. "No way," he said. "Mark never goes to the net, and even if Blanca's plenty strong, she's wild when she's nervous. Besides, remember what Suzy says: 'A positive mental attitude counts big time'—so think positive! Anyway, this isn't Wimbledon; we're supposed to go out there and have fun."

It didn't feel like much fun when Blanca and Mark won the toss and chose to serve first. Emily assumed the ready position in the forehand court and tried to prepare for the first serve

Mark would blast at her. She barely saw the ball as it zipped over the net, but she stuck out her racket, stepped into the ball and surprised everyone by hitting a winner.

"Awesome," Eric whispered.

"Beginner's luck," Emily whispered back. "Your turn." She could hear her mother cheering from the hill beside the courts, but she didn't really mind.

The two pairs were evenly matched, and the score nudged forward point by point. The set went on for forty minutes, until the score was tied at six games apiece.

"Perfect," Suzy said. "Now we get to see a real tie-breaker. Blanca, your serve."

Blanca smiled, but Emily was perplexed to see that Eric looked panic-stricken as he prepared to receive the serve. Blanca hit the ball squarely, and Eric missed it by a wide margin.

"Eric, what is it?" she croaked. "You

barely even took a swing."

He looked at her dejectedly.

"The tie-breaker," he whispered. "I don't know how to call the score."

Emily barely had time to think.

"Just watch me," she said. "I'll use my fingers to flash you the score behind my back. Just think of it all as points; the first pair to get seven points wins. There's no deuce, no ads, no nothing. Plain old numbers, and right now we're behind 0-1. Let's get going."

But they didn't get going. Blanca and Mark took the next five points in a row, which left Eric and Emily behind at 6-0 when it was Emily's turn to serve.

"Now or never," she told herself as she held the ball steady in front of her.

"Ace," Suzy called as the class watched in disbelief when Blanca failed to even connect with the ball Emily had served.

"One-6," Emily said sternly as she

moved to the backhand court and pre-pared to serve to Mark.

Mark was ready for her, however, and the ball zipped back over the net—to Emily's backhand. She felt her heart clutch, and she stared blindly as the ball fired into her racket then dribbled pitifully into the net.

A cheer went up from the crowd, and Mark and Blanca lifted their rackets skyward in the glow of victory. She turned to Eric.

He shrugged and smiled. "Good effort, Wilson," he said. "Heck, we'll get them next time!"

The sting of defeat was forgotten as everyone gathered for strawberries and sparkling cider.

"I don't get it," Eric said. "What are the strawberries for, anyway?"

"Wimbledon," Emily said. "It's just like Wimbledon."

Eric became very quiet and dreamy-eyed. "Yeah, well I'm going there someday," he said.

Emily nodded. "Me, too. But first, I think maybe I need a few more lessons."

"Yeah, I know what you mean. I signed up for the next session, except Suzy moved me up to intermediate." He sounded a little disappointed.

"Really?" Emily said with a grin. "Me, too."